Is there a way home through the blizzard?

It seemed to be growing colder by the minute. The snow, blown by the wind, was beginning to drift along the north side of the street. Only a few people were making their way up Third Avenue.

"Maybe we should go back home, Grandpa," Anna said. "I don't think I care so much now about that spelling competition."

"Of course you care, Anna! And I'm going to see that you get to school."

"But Grandpa, the wind is getting so strong I can hardly walk."

"You don't have to walk. We'll go by train."

Anna looked up. It was snowing so hard that she could barely see the train tracks of the Third Avenue overhead line above her.

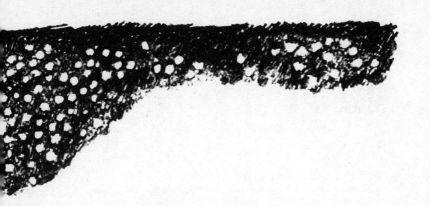

CARLA STEVENS

Anna, Grandpa, and the Big Storm

ILLUSTRATED BY MARGOT TOMES

PUFFIN BOOKS

For Marie
    C. S.

PUFFIN BOOKS
Published by the Penguin Group
Penguin Putnam Inc., 375 Hudson Street, New York, New York 10014, U.S.A.
Penguin Books Ltd, 27 Wrights Lane, London W8 5TZ, England
Penguin Books Australia Ltd, Ringwood, Victoria, Australia
Penguin Books Canada Ltd, 10 Alcorn Avenue, Toronto, Ontario, Canada M4V 3B2
Penguin Books (N.Z.) Ltd, 182-190 Wairau Road, Auckland 10, New Zealand

Penguin Books Ltd, Registered Offices: Harmondsworth, Middlesex, England

First published in the United States of America by Clarion Books, 1982
Reprinted by arrangement with Houghton Mifflin Company
First published in Great Britain by Penguin Books Ltd, 1984
Published in Puffin Books (U.K.), 1985
Published in Puffin Books (U.S.A.), 1986
Reissued 1998

30 29 28 27 26

Text copyright © Carla Stevens, 1982
Illustrations copyright © Margot Tomes, 1982
All rights reserved

LIBRARY OF CONGRESS CATALOGING-IN-PUBLICATION DATA
Stevens, Carla.
Anna, Grandpa, and the big storm / Carla Stevens; illustrated by Margot Tomes.
    p. cm.—(Puffin chapters)
Summary: Anna's grandfather is bored with city life until he and Anna are stranded
on the Third Avenue elevated subway train during the blizzard of 1888.
ISBN 0-14-130083-3 (pbk.)
[1. Grandfathers—Fiction. 2. Blizzards—New York (State)—New York—Fiction.
3.New York (N.Y.)—History—1865–1898—Fiction.]
I. Tomes, Margot, ill. II. Title. III. Series.
PZ7.S8435An 1998 [E]—DC21 97-50525 CIP AC

Printed in the United States of America

RL: 2.3

Contents

I

Grandpa Comes to Visit

Anna sat at the kitchen table trying to study her spelling words. But it was no use. Grandpa was making a fuss again.

'I want to go home,' he said.

'You have only been here three days,' Anna's father replied. 'I will take you home next Saturday.'

'I can't wait that long,' said Grandpa.

Mrs Romano looked at her father sternly. 'Now see here, Papa. Next time when we invite you, you can say "no". But this time you said "yes". And that's why you are here.'

Grandpa frowned. 'There's nothing for me to do in the city,' he said. 'Especially on a rainy day.'

'Don't you like us, Grandpa?' Tony asked.

Grandpa Jensen looked down at his young grandson. 'Of course I do, Tony. I just can't stand being cooped up like a hen.'

Anna pushed her chair back and stood up. How could she get her homework done with Grandpa fussing and stewing all week? She walked to the living-room and looked out of the window on to Fifteenth Street. Not even the haloes of light cast by the gas lamps could brighten this dreary Sunday.

Grandpa came and stood behind her. 'Past time for milking. Never thought I'd miss the farm so,' he said softly.

For a moment Anna felt sorry for her grandfather. But then he started grumbling again. 'How a man can live in a city like this is more than I can understand.'

Later, when Anna was in bed, Mama came to kiss her good night. 'Grandpa fusses a lot,' Anna whispered.

'I know,' said her mother. 'I invited Grandpa to visit us. I thought it would be a change for him after your grandmother died.'

'He isn't polite,' Anna said.

Anna's mother smiled. 'Your grandfather has always said just what he thinks.'

Anna sighed. 'Still I wish he liked it better here.'

'You must try to make him feel at home, Anna. He's an old man.'

'Yes, Mama.'

'Now go to sleep.' Mama kissed her on the forehead. She closed the door quietly behind her.

Anna tried to think what she could do to make Grandpa feel more at home. She and Tony could take him for a walk to Washington Square Park. They could show him the grey squirrel's nest in the big oak tree near the arch, and the daffodils already in bloom around the fountain.

Anna listened to the sleet hitting the skylight above her head. 'Oh, I hope tomorrow will be a nice day,' she thought just before she fell asleep.

2

Snow in the Morning

When Anna woke up she thought it was still night. No light came through the skylight. She turned on her side in bed and looked through the doorway into the kitchen. Tony was at the table eating his porridge. Grandpa was pouring a bucketful of coal into the big stove.

Anna jumped out of bed and ran into the kitchen to get dressed. Mama came in from the living-room.

'What time is it, Mama?' Anna

asked, warming her hands over the hot stove.

'Almost seven thirty,' Mama said. 'Go to the front window and see what is happening outside.'

Anna looked out of the window. It was snowing so hard, she could

scarcely see the houses across the street.

'Don't worry, it won't last,' Grandpa said. 'After all, it's almost the middle of March.'

Mama put a bowl of porridge on the table for Anna. 'Maybe you should stay home from school today,' she said.

'I can't, Mama. Today is the last day of the spelling competition. If I win, I'll be in the City Finals.'

Mrs Romano sighed. 'If Papa were here, he could take you.'

'Where is Papa?' Anna asked.

'He left very early to take his new harnesses to the trolley-bus station in Harlem.'

'What's the matter with me?' Grandpa asked. 'Why can't I take her? Besides, I want to stop at Mr Knudsen's shop and get some more tobacco.'

'But I want to walk to school by myself, the way I always do,' Anna said.

Grandpa gave Anna a sad look. 'It's no fun when you're old.' He shook his head. 'No one thinks you're good for anything.'

'I don't think that, Grandpa,' Anna said quickly.

'But it's snowing hard outside,

Papa,' Anna's mother said.

'Do you think I've never seen snow before?' Grandpa asked. 'Anna's going to school, and I'm going to take her. And that's that!'

'All right, all right, go along you two,' Mama said. 'But take the over-head railway, Anna. Then you won't have to walk such a long way.'

Grandpa put on his overcoat and his hat with ear flaps and his big galoshes.

'And be sure to come straight back if school is closed,' Anna's mother added.

'We will,' Anna said. 'Goodbye, Mama. Goodbye, Tony.'

'Come on, Anna,' Grandpa said cheerfully. 'Let's see what your city looks like in the snow!'

3

Out with Grandpa

As soon as Anna started down the front
steps, she knew something was different
about this snow. It was not falling
down. It was blowing sideways,
pricking her face like sharp needles.
She pulled her scarf up over her nose.

Anna and Grandpa plodded down
the street. The wind whipped the snow
in great swirls around them as they
crossed Broadway and tramped
through Union Square. When they
reached the fire station, Anna saw a

fireman shovelling snow away from the stable doors.

'Morning!' Grandpa said brightly. 'Quite a storm for this time of year!'

'It caught us by surprise,' the fireman replied. 'Where are you going on a day like this?'

'To school,' Grandpa said. 'My granddaughter, Anna, is in the final of the spelling competition.'

'Good luck to you, little lassie,' the fireman said.

Anna pulled her scarf down from her mouth so she could say 'thank you'. But she felt embarrassed. She didn't like it when Grandpa talked about her to strangers.

They finally reached the corner of Fifteenth Street and Third Avenue. Grandpa turned the door handle of Mr Knudsen's tobacco shop. But the door

wouldn't open.

Anna cleared a spot on the window with her mitten and peered inside. It was dark.

'What kind of shopkeeper is he?' Grandpa grumbled. 'He doesn't even come to work!'

'But Grandpa, it's snowing hard now.'

'Child, do you think the world stands still every time it snows?' Grandpa looked at her crossly.

It seemed to be growing colder by the minute. The snow, blown by the wind, was beginning to drift along the north side of the street. Only a few people were making their way up Third Avenue.

'Maybe we should go back home, Grandpa,' Anna said. 'I don't think I care so much now about that spelling competition.'

'Of course you care, Anna! And I'm going to see that you get to school.'

'But Grandpa, the wind is getting so strong I can hardly walk.' Anna tried not to sound frightened.

'You don't have to walk. We'll do

just what your mother suggested. We'll
go by train.'

Anna looked up. It was snowing so
hard that she could barely see the train
tracks of the Third Avenue overhead
line above her.

4

The Third Avenue Railway

Anna followed Grandpa up the long flight of steps to the Fourteenth Street station. No one was at the ticket-office so they ducked under the turnstile to the platform. They stood out of the wind at the head of the stairs. Anna could see only one other person waiting for a train on the up platform.

Anna looked at her rosy-cheeked grandfather. Snow clung to his moustache and eyebrows and froze. They looked like tiny icebergs.

'Here comes the train!' Grandpa shouted.

A steam engine, pulling two green carriages, puffed towards them. When the train stopped, Anna and Grandpa hurried across the platform and stepped inside. There were lots of empty seats. They sat down behind a large woman. She took up most of the seat in front of them.

Anna pulled off her hat. Her pompom looked like a big white snowball. She shook it, spraying the floor with wet snow. The guard came up the aisle and stopped at their seat.

Grandpa said, 'No one was at the station to sell us a ticket.'

'That will be five cents,' the guard said. 'Each.'

'You mean I have to pay for her, too?' Grandpa's eyes twinkled.

'Grandpa,' Anna whispered, tugging
at his arm. 'I'm almost eight years old.'

Grandpa and the guard laughed.
Anna didn't like to be teased. She
turned away and tried to look out, but
snow covered the windows.

Grandpa leaned forward. 'Quite a

storm,' he said to the woman in the
seat in front of them. 'Nothing like the
Blizzard of '72, though. Why, it was so
cold, the smoke froze as it came out of
the chimney!'

There he goes again, Anna thought.
Why does Grandpa always talk to
strangers?

A woman holding a basket sat across

from them. She leaned over. 'In Poland, when I was a little girl, it snowed like this all winter long.'

The woman in the seat in front turned around. 'This storm can't last. The first day of spring is less than two weeks away.'

'That's just what I was telling my daughter this morning!' Grandpa said.

Anna could see that Grandpa was growing more cheerful by the minute.

Suddenly the train stopped.

'What's the trouble?' the woman from Poland asked. 'Guard, why has the train stopped?'

The guard didn't reply. He opened the carriage door and stepped out on to the platform. No one inside said a word.

Then Grandpa stood up. 'I'll find out what's the matter.'

Anna tugged at his coat sleeve. 'Oh, please sit down, Grandpa.' He didn't seem to understand how scared she felt. How she wished she had stayed home!

The door opened again and the guard entered the carriage. He was covered with snow. 'We're stuck,' he said. 'The engine can't move. Too much snow has drifted on to the tracks ahead. We'll have to stay here until help comes.'

'Did you hear that, Anna?' Grandpa almost bounced up and down in his seat. 'We're stuck! Stuck and stranded on the overhead railway! What do you think about that!'

5

Stranded

When Anna heard the news, she grew even more frightened. 'Mama will be so worried. She doesn't know where we are.'

'She knows you are with me,' Grandpa said cheerfully. 'That's all she needs to know.' He leaned forward again. 'We might as well get acquainted,' he said. 'My name is Erik Jensen, and this is my granddaughter, Anna.'

The woman in the seat in front turned around. 'Josie Sweeney,' she

said. 'Pleased to meet you.'

'How-dee-do,' said the woman across the aisle. 'I'm Mrs Esther Polanski. And this is my friend, Miss Ruth Cohen.'

Someone tapped Anna on her shoulder. She turned around. Two

young men smiled. One of them said,
'John King and my brother, Bruce.'

A young woman with a high fur
collar and a big hat sat by herself at the
rear of the carriage. Anna looked in
her direction. 'My name is Anna
Romano,' she said shyly. 'I'm Addie
Beaver,' said the young woman. She
smiled and wrapped her coat more
tightly around her.

It was growing colder and colder inside the carriage. When the guard shook the snow off his clothes, it no longer melted into puddles on the floor.

'We'll all freeze to death if we stay here,' moaned Mrs Sweeney.

'Oooooo, my feet are so cold,' Addie Beaver said.

Anna looked at her high-buttoned shoes and felt sorry for Addie Beaver.

Even though Anna had on her warm boots, her toes began to grow cold, too. She stood in the aisle and stamped her feet up and down.

Suddenly Anna had an idea. 'Grandpa!' she said. 'I know a game we can play that might help keep us warm.'

'Why Anna, what a good idea,' Grandpa replied.

'It's called "Simon Says".'

'Listen everybody!' Grandpa shouted. 'My granddaughter, Anna, knows a game that will help us stay warm.'

'How do we play, Anna?' asked Mrs Polanski. 'Tell us.'

'Everybody has to stand up,' said Anna.

'Come on, everybody,' Grandpa said. 'We must keep moving if we don't want to freeze to death.'

Miss Beaver was the first to stand.
Then John and Bruce King stood up.
Grandpa bowed first to Mrs Sweeney,
then to Mrs Polanski and Miss Cohen.
'May I help you, ladies?' he asked.
They giggled and stood up. Now
everybody was looking at Anna.

'All right,' she said. 'You must do
only what Simon tells you to do. If *I*
tell you to do something, you mustn't
do it.'

'I don't understand,' Mrs Sweeney
said.

'Maybe we'll catch on if we start
playing,' Grandpa said.

'All right,' Anna said. 'I'll begin.
Simon says, "Clap your hands."'

Everybody began to clap hands.

'Simon says, "Stop!"'

Everybody stopped.

'Good!' Anna said. 'Simon says,
"Follow me!"' Anna marched down
the aisle of the carriage, then around
one of the handrails, then back again.
Everyone followed her.

'Simon says, "Stop!"'

Everyone stopped.

Anna patted her head and rubbed
her stomach at the same time.

'Simon says, "Pat your head and rub

your stomach." Like this.'

Everyone began to laugh at one another.

'Simon says, "Swing your arms around and around."'

'Ooof! This is hard work!' puffed Mrs Sweeney.

'Now. Touch your toes!'

Mrs Sweeney bent down and tried to touch her toes.

'Oh! Oh! You're out, Mrs Sweeney!' Anna said.

'Why am I out?' She asked indignantly.

Anna giggled. 'Because *Simon* didn't say to touch your toes. *I* did!'

Mrs Sweeney sat down. 'It's just as well,' she panted. 'I was getting all tired out.'

'Is everyone warming up?' Grandpa asked.

'Yes! Yes!' they all shouted.

Snow was sifting like flour through the cracks around the windows. Just then, the door opened. A blast of icy cold air blew into the carriage. Everyone shivered. It was the guard coming back in again.

'Get ready to leave,' he said. 'The firemen are coming!'

6

Firemen to the Rescue

Everyone rushed to the door and tried to look out. The snow stung Anna's eyes. The wind almost took her breath away.

The guard closed the door again quickly. 'The wind is so fierce it's going to be hard to get a ladder up this high. We're at least ten metres above Third Avenue.'

Ladder! Ten metres! Anna shivered.

'Oh, Lord help me,' groaned Mrs Sweeney. 'I'll never be able to climb down a ladder.' She gave Grandpa a pleading look.

'Oh yes you will, Mrs Sweeney,' he said. 'Once you get the hang of it, it's easy.'

'In all that wind?' Mrs Sweeney said. 'Never!'

'Don't worry, Mrs Sweeney. You won't blow away,' said Grandpa.

Anna looked at Grandpa. 'I'm scared too,' she said.

'And what about me?' asked Mrs Polanski. 'I can't stand heights.'

The door opened and a fireman appeared. He shook the snow off his clothes. 'We'll take you down one at a time. Who wants to go first?'

No one spoke.

'Anna,' said Grandpa. 'You're a brave girl. You go first.'

'I'm afraid to climb down the ladder, Grandpa.'

'Why Anna, I'm surprised at you. Don't you remember how you climbed down from the hayloft last summer? It was easy.'

'You can do it, Anna,' said Miss Cohen.

'Pretend we're still playing that

game. Simon says, "Go down the ladder",' said Mrs Sweeney.

'So go now,' Miss Cohen said. 'We'll see you below.'

'I'll be right below you to shield you from the wind. You won't fall,' said the fireman.

Anna shook with fear. She didn't want to be first to go down the ladder. But how could she disappoint the others?

Grandpa opened the door. The guard held her hand. Anna put first one foot, then the other, on the ladder. The fierce wind pulled her and pushed her. Icy snow stuck to her clothes, weighing her down.

The fireman was below her on the ladder. His strong arms were around her, holding her steady. With her left foot, Anna felt for the rung below.

Step by step by step, she cautiously went down the ladder. Thirty steps. Would she never reach the bottom? One foot plunged into the snow and then the other. Oh, so much snow! It covered her legs and reached almost to her waist.

'Stay close to the engine until the rest are down,' the fireman said.

Anna struggled through the deep snow to the fire engine. The horses, whipped by the icy wind and snow, stood still, their heads low. Anna huddled against the side of the engine. The roar of the storm was growing louder.

7

The Storm Grows
Worse

First came Mrs Polanski, then Ruth
Cohen. Then Bruce and John King.
Then Addie Beaver. One at a time, the
fireman helped each person down the
ladder. Now only Grandpa and Mrs
Sweeney remained to be rescued.

Anna could see two shapes on the
ladder, one behind the other. The
fireman was bringing down someone
else.

'Oh, I hope it's Grandpa,' Anna said
to Addie Beaver.

Suddenly she gasped. She could

hardly believe her eyes. One minute the two shapes were there. The next minute they weren't!

Everyone struggled through the deep snow to find out who had fallen off the ladder.

Anna was first to reach the fireman who was brushing snow off his clothes. 'What happened?' she asked.

'Mrs Sweeney missed a step on the ladder. Down she went, taking me with her,' the fireman replied.

Mrs Sweeney lay sprawled in the snow nearby. Her arms and legs were spread out, as if she were going to make a snow angel.

'Are you all right, Mrs Sweeney?' Grandpa asked. Anna had not seen Grandpa come down the ladder by himself. Now he stood beside her.

'I'm just fine, Mr Jensen. I think I'm

going to lie right here until the storm is
over.'

'Oh no you're not!' Grandpa said.
He and a fireman each took one of Mrs
Sweeney's arms. They pulled her to her
feet.

49

Anna couldn't help giggling. Now Mrs Sweeney looked like a giant snow lady!

'Climb on to the engine,' said a fire-man. 'We must get the horses back to the fire station. The temperature is dropping fast.'

'We live quite near here,' Mrs Polanski and Miss Cohen said. 'We're going to try to get home.'

'We'll see that you get there,' John King said. 'We live in Lafayette Street.' The young men and the two ladies linked arms and trudged off through the snow.

'What about you, Miss Beaver?' Grandpa asked. She looked confused.

'Hey, this is no tea party! Let's go!' said the fireman.

'You come with us then, Miss

Beaver,' Grandpa said. 'You too, Mrs Sweeney.'

Anna's fingers were numb with cold. She could hardly hold on to the railing of the engine. Often she had seen the horses racing down the street to a fire. Now they plodded along very, very slowly through the deep snow.

No one spoke. The wind roared and shrieked. The snow blinded them. One fireman jumped off the engine and tried to lead the horses forward.

Anna huddled against the side of the engine, hiding her face in her arms. It was taking them such a long time to reach the fire station.

Just then, the horses turned abruptly to the left. The next moment they were inside the stable, snorting and stamping their hooves.

Several men ran forward to unhitch the engine. Everyone began brushing the icy snow off their clothes.

Suddenly Grandpa became very serious. 'The thermometer says five degrees above zero, and the temperature is still dropping. We must get home as fast as possible. Mrs Sweeney, you and Miss Beaver had better come with us.'

'Here, Miss,' a fireman said. 'Put these boots on. You can return them when the storm is over.'

'Oh, thank you,' Addie Beaver said.

Anna had forgotten about Addie's high-buttoned shoes.

'Whatever you do, Anna, you are *not* to let go of my hand.' Grandpa spoke firmly.

'Mr Jensen, would you mind if I

held your other hand?' asked Mrs
Sweeney.

'Not a bit,' said Grandpa. 'Anna,
you take hold of Miss Beaver's hand.
No one is to let go under *any*
circumstances. Do you all understand?'

Anna had never heard Grandpa talk
like that before. Was he frightened too?

They plunged into the deep snow,
moving slowly along the south side of
Fifteenth Street. The wind had piled
the snow into huge drifts on the north
side of the street.

When they reached Broadway, the
wind was blowing up the avenue with
the force of a hurricane. Telephone
and telegraph wires were down.
Thousands of them cut through the air
like whips. If only they could reach the
other side, Anna thought. Then they

would be only a short way from home.

No one spoke. They clung to one
another as they blindly made their way
across the avenue. Mrs Sweeney lost

her balance and fell forward in the
snow. For a moment Anna thought she
was there to stay. But Grandpa tugged
at her arm and helped her get to her
feet.

They trudged on until they reached the other side. Now to find their house. How lucky they were to live on the south side of the street. The snow had reached as high as the first-floor windows of the houses on the north side. At last they came to Number 44.

Up the seven steps they climbed. Then through the front door and up more stairs. A moment later, Mr Romano opened the door of their flat. 'Papa, you're home,' Anna cried, and fell into her father's arms.

8

Home at Last!

Several hours later, Anna sat in the
kitchen watching a game of draughts.
Mrs Sweeney, wearing Grandpa's
dressing-gown, was playing draughts
with Grandpa, while Miss Beaver, in
Mama's clothes, chatted with Mama.
Outside, the storm whistled and
roared. Tomorrow would be time
enough to study her spelling, Anna
decided. Now she just wanted to enjoy
the company.

Suddenly Grandpa pushed his chair

back. 'You win, Mrs Sweeney. Where did you learn to play draughts?'

'I belong to a club,' Mrs Sweeney replied. 'I'm the champ. We meet every Tuesday. Maybe you will come with me next Tuesday, Mr Jensen?'

'Why, I'd like that,' answered Grandpa.

'You can't, Grandpa,' Tony said. 'You're going home on Saturday.'

'Who says so?' Grandpa asked.

'You did. Don't you remember?'

'Hush, Tony,' Anna said. 'Maybe he will stay a little longer. I think Grandpa likes the city better now.'

Mrs Romano smiled. 'It took a snowstorm to change his mind.'

'You call this a snowstorm?' said Grandpa. He winked at Anna. 'When you are an old lady, Anna, as old as I

am now, you will be telling your
grandchildren all about our adventure
in The Great Blizzard of 1888!'

The Great Blizzard of 1888

There really *was* a great blizzard in America in 1888. It began to snow early on Monday morning, March 12th. Before the snow stopped on Tuesday, over a metre had fallen in New York City. Nearly two metres fell in Boston and in other parts of the east.

The winds blew at 75 miles an hour and piled the snow in huge drifts. Everywhere, people were stranded. In New York City, about 15,000 people were trapped in trains on the overhead railway. Like Anna and Grandpa, they had to be rescued by firemen with ladders.

By Thursday of that same week, the sun was out again. The snow began to melt. Anna went to school and won the spelling competition. And Grandpa walked down to Sullivan Street to play draughts again with Josie Sweeney.

OTHER CHAPTER BOOKS FROM PUFFIN